Barbie™

MYSTERY FILES #4

The Mystery of the Missing Stallion

W9-ACI-983

Want to read more of Barbie's Mystery Files? Don't miss the first three books in the series, The Haunted Mansion Mystery, The Mystery of the Jeweled Mask, and Mystery Unplugged.

Barbie™

MYSTERY FILES #4

The Mystery of the Missing Stallion

By Linda Williams Aber

SCHOLASTIC INC.

New York   Toronto   London   Auckland   Sydney
Mexico City   New Delhi   Hong Kong   Buenos Aires

If you purchased this book without a cover, you should be aware that this book is stolen property. It was reported as "unsold and destroyed" to the publisher, and neither the author nor the publisher has received any payment for this "stripped book."

No part of this publication may be reproduced in whole or in part, or stored in a retrieval system, or transmitted in any form or by any means, electronic, mechanical, photocopying, recording, or otherwise, without written permission of the publisher. For information regarding permission, write to Scholastic Inc., Attention: Permissions Department, 557 Broadway, New York, NY 10012.

ISBN 0-439-37207-0

BARBIE and associated trademarks are owned by and used under license from Mattel, Inc.
Copyright © 2002 Mattel, Inc. All Rights Reserved.
Published by Scholastic Inc.
SCHOLASTIC and associated logos are trademarks and/or registered trademarks of Scholastic Inc.

Designed by Peter Koblish
Photography by Tom Wolfson, Shirley Oshirogata, Jake Johnson, Jeremy Lloyd, Steve Toth, Judy Tsuno, and Lisa Collins

12 11 10 9 8 7 6 5 4 3 2   2 3 4 5 6/0

Printed in the U.S.A.
First Scholastic printing, September 2002

You can help Barbie solve this mystery! Flip to page 64 and use the reporter's notebook to jot down facts, clues, and suspects in the case. Add more notes as you and Barbie uncover clues. If you can figure out who the culprit is, you'll be on your way to becoming a star reporter, just like Barbie!

Barbie™

MYSTERY FILES #4

The Mystery of the Missing Stallion

Chapter 1

• • • • • • • • • • • • • • • • • • •

STAR ASSIGNMENT

"There's your bag, Teresa!" Barbie called out as a green suitcase glided toward the two friends. Barbie stood on tiptoe in the Albuquerque, New Mexico, airport, waiting for the baggage carousel to bring their luggage around. She reached across and grabbed the handle of Teresa's suitcase, struggling a bit to lift it onto the floor. "Whoa!" she said, laughing. "Did you pack horseshoes along with your riding clothes? This weighs a ton!"

Teresa blushed. "Oh, Barbie," she said. "I guess I did bring a few too many shoes of my own. I just wasn't sure what shoes I'd need on a dude ranch, so I brought them all! Luckily, this suitcase has wheels."

"Mine does, too," Barbie replied. "And here it

1

comes now!" A bright red suitcase with a matching red luggage tag came toward them. Barbie was about to reach for it when another hand came forward and easily lifted the bag off the carousel.

"I'll get that for you, Ms. Roberts," a man in a chauffeur's uniform said. He smiled as he put the suitcase down at Barbie's feet.

"Wow!" Teresa exclaimed. "That's really star treatment! Is it because you're a reporter?"

"Star Canyon Ranch welcomes you," the man said. "I'm Ralph, and I'll be your driver to the ranch." The pleasant-looking man showed the two girls his identification badge.

"Thank you, Ralph," Barbie said. "And this is my friend Teresa. We'll both be staying for the week."

"It's going to be some week at the ranch," Ralph said, leading the girls to the limousine. "There's a whole crowd of movie folks there already."

"Movie folks?" Teresa asked, bewildered. She looked at her friend.

Barbie had a twinkle in her eye. She had a surprise for Teresa and was bursting to tell her.

"What?" Teresa asked. She and Barbie had been

friends since kindergarten. She knew Barbie very well, and she was sure that her friend was up to something. "Why are you smiling like that? What's going on?"

"Okay, okay." Barbie finally gave up. "I wasn't going to tell you until we actually got to the ranch, but I can't keep the secret any longer. We — that is, you and I," Barbie said excitedly, "are *not* here just for a vacation at the Star Canyon Ranch. And we're *not* here just to go horseback riding. We're here because the *Willow Gazette* is doing an exclusive behind-the-scenes story on the filming of the new movie *Riding on the Wind.* I'll be reporting on it for the newspaper!"

"Oh, my gosh!" Teresa exclaimed.

Barbie laughed. "We're going to meet the cast and get an up-close look at what it's like to film a movie on location — that means filming in a real place, not just inside a studio."

Teresa's face lit up. "I saw one of the actors from *Riding on the Wind* on a television show yesterday!"

"Maybe you saw the actor I brought out to the ranch this morning," Ralph said. "He was here all

3

last week but had to go to California to do a television interview. Have you heard of Matt Carson?"

"That's him! That's who I saw," Teresa said.

Barbie was beaming. "Matt Carson and the rest of the movie crew are staying at the Star Canyon Ranch." She reached into her tote bag and pulled out a publicity folder from the movie. Inside was a glossy photo of Matt Carson. "And you're right that he's in the movie, but his costar is getting even more attention. His name is Orion and he's a —"

"Horse!" Teresa said, finishing Barbie's sentence. "I know all about Orion. I've been following his career ever since he won the big derby two years ago. That horse is a real legend, even if he is retired from racing now."

Barbie smiled at her friend. Teresa had always loved horses. She had won a wall full of ribbons for horse shows she'd been in. That was exactly why Barbie had invited Teresa to come along on this assignment.

"This is going to be so incredible!" Teresa said. "I don't know which I'm more excited about — seeing a *human* movie star or seeing a *horse* movie star!"

"Well," Ralph put in, "I guess we'd better get going if you want to see any of the stars, human or horse!" He led the way to the waiting limousine and opened the door for the two friends. After loading their luggage into the trunk, he took his place behind the wheel. "Sit back, relax, and enjoy the ride. It's about an hour away, but we'll be there in time to see the sunset."

As the long black limo headed away from the airport and toward the red clay hills, Barbie took out her reporter's notebook and made the first entry for her new assignment: *Star Canyon Ranch — location for* Riding on the Wind, *starring Matt Carson and Orion.*

Ralph pointed out sites of interest along the route leading to the ranch, and Barbie filled in Teresa on their plans. "Tonight we'll just get settled, have an early dinner, and go to bed. We'll need to be fresh and ready for a long day on the set of the movie. In the morning, Sam Rogan, the assistant director, is going to meet us and we'll watch a scene being filmed."

"Yes," Ralph added. "I think they will be back in

production by morning. You know, they had a flood in one of the equipment storage places and that delayed things for a couple of days."

"A flood?" Barbie said. "That's too bad!"

"Well, it was just equipment that got damaged. Luckily, no one was hurt. Some think it may have been a publicity stunt to draw attention to the movie."

"That seems like it would be going a little too far just for publicity," Barbie said.

"You're right," Ralph agreed. "And thank goodness nothing happened to that horse. If anything happened to Orion, that would be publicity *nobody* wants. Seems like nothing matters more than keeping that horse safe and happy. He's insured for millions of dollars, but of course money couldn't replace a champion like Orion. Yes, they've had more than their fair share of trouble on the set," Ralph continued. "But I'm sure it'll all be fine for your visit."

Conversation continued, and nobody noticed the rusty green pickup truck speeding up behind them. It wasn't until they felt the limousine swerve suddenly and heard Ralph shouting, "Hey! Watch where you're going!" that they paid any attention to the road.

Barbie looked out and saw that they were headed right for a giant boulder! "Oh, no!" she cried. "We're going to crash!"

The heavy limousine bump, bump, bumped onto the side of the country road. Finally, it came to a lumbering halt in a patch of scruffy sagebrush. The green pickup roared away.

"Whew!" Barbie said, straightening up in her seat. "That was close!"

"Are you two all right?" Ralph asked.

No one was hurt, but they were shaken by the incident.

"He ran us right off the road!" Teresa exclaimed.

"He sure did," Ralph said, righting his cap on his head. "And I'm afraid we've got a flat tire because of it. Sorry, ladies, but you'll have to get out while I change it."

The girls got out of the limousine. As Ralph worked to change the flat, Barbie realized that no other cars were on the road. The sun was already setting and the night air was turning cool. "I'm glad it was only a flat tire," she said.

"Okay," Ralph said, putting the jack and the blown tire into the trunk. "We're all set. Let's try this again."

"I can't believe the driver of that truck didn't even look back," Teresa said when they were driving again. "He must know he ran us off the road."

"I can tell you one thing," Ralph said. "There was plenty of room for both of us on the road. I hate to say it, but whoever it was knew exactly what he was doing!"

The thought of what could have happened silenced both Barbie and Teresa. Thankfully, the rest of the ride was uneventful. The sun had set, and they stopped along the way for a light dinner. When they finally reached the Star Canyon Ranch, it looked as if the whole place was locked up for the night. Lights were on in individual guest houses, but there was no activity outside.

"People go to bed early here," Ralph explained, "because of the early film call in the morning." He delivered them to the door of a guest house that had been assigned to them, carried their luggage inside, and said good-night.

Tired from their long day of travel, Barbie and

Teresa quickly washed up and climbed into their beds.

"Good night, Barbie," Teresa said sleepily, closing her eyes.

"Good night, Teresa," Barbie replied, her eyes still open and her mind going over the events of the day. She took out her reporter's notebook and added to her notes.

Trouble at Star Canyon Ranch — flood damages equipment.
Trouble on the way to ranch — green pickup truck runs limo off the road.

"Barbie?" Teresa said after a minute. "Why would anyone want to do something like that?"

"I don't know, Teresa," Barbie said softly. "That's exactly what I'd like to know, and before we leave, I plan to find out!" Before turning out the light, Barbie added one more line to her notes.

Questions: Who? Why?

Chapter 2

● ● ● ● ● ● ● ● ● ● ● ● ● ● ● ● ● ● ● ●

AN ASSIGNMENT IN
AN ASSIGNMENT

MOOoooo. . . . MOOoooo. . . .

Barbie's eyes flew open. She looked across at Teresa in the bed opposite hers and waited to hear the sound again.

MOOooo. . . . MOOooo.

Suddenly, Barbie started laughing. The sound wasn't coming from her friend. It was coming from outside! She remembered where they were and jumped out of bed to look out the window. "Teresa!" Barbie exclaimed. "Wake up and look!"

"Oh," Teresa said sleepily. "Is it morning already?"

"No." Barbie laughed. "It isn't morning, it's MOO-rning! Come here and look at the cows!"

Teresa ran to the back window and stood next

to her friend. "Oh, my gosh!" she gasped when she saw the open field dotted with grazing cows. "I can't believe we're really here! After the excitement of the accident I was so tired, I couldn't even look around the room last night. Let's get dressed. I want to explore a little."

"And I want to explore *a lot,*" Barbie said eagerly. She was already taking her first good look around. The girls were in a big room with two double beds, a living area with sofa and chairs, and a separate bath. The walls were sand-colored with dark wood beams on the ceiling. Splashes of turquoise on the rug, guest towels, bedspreads, and curtains at the front and back windows added just the right amount of color to the lodge.

"It's perfect!" Teresa said, admiring the paintings of wild horses that hung on the walls over the beds.

Barbie opened the front windows to let in fresh air. Along with the air came the sound of shouting from the corral area. "Hey!" she said. "Something's going on over there already. Let's get ready and walk over."

They rushed to shower and dress. Leaving the

11

unpacking for later, they followed the paved road around to the field, where the film crew and all their equipment was. Parked behind the barns were trailers marked with the Silvertone Studios logo. Some were used for storage of costumes, sets, props, and equipment. Others were obviously being used for dressing rooms, makeup rooms, and actors' rest areas. Set back from the trailers was a stable with a silver-and-black horse trailer parked next to it. The name Orion was written on both sides of the fancy trailer in bright blue letters.

"Wow," Teresa exclaimed. "Orion has the nicest trailer of all!"

"I guess that's what a star's dressing room looks like when the star is a horse." Barbie giggled.

"I can't wait to see him!" Teresa said.

"Well, maybe I can help you with that," a voice said from behind them.

The girls turned and came face-to-face with a good-looking young man with blond hair and brown eyes. "Good morning!" Barbie said, smiling. "I'm —"

"Barbie Roberts, reporter for the *Willow Gazette*,"

the young man finished. "And this must be your friend Teresa, right?" He introduced himself. "Sam Rogan, assistant director, at your service. Sorry I wasn't there to greet you last night. It was a busy day and you were late arriving."

"It's good to meet you, Sam," Barbie said. "We came over to have a look around, and we were just about to look for you."

"I found you first," Sam said, smiling. "I trust you had a smooth flight and that Ralph took good care of you."

Barbie and Teresa exchanged looks, and Barbie quickly spoke. "Yes, we had a great flight, and Ralph was there to meet us right on time. There was a little accident on the way here, but we're all right."

"Accident?" Sam asked, looking concerned.

Barbie explained about the truck running them off the road, and Sam shook his head. "I can't believe it," he said. "I only hope that's the last of the trouble now. We don't need anything else happening on this movie shoot."

"Anything else?" Barbie asked, raising her eyebrow.

13

"Barbie, can I tell you something off the record?" Sam asked, looking serious.

"Of course," Barbie said. "If you tell me it's off the record, I won't use it in my article."

"Well," Sam began, "since you were involved in the latest incident, it's only fair to warn you that there could be more trouble. Someone has been working overtime to ruin this project. At first, little things went wrong — scripts were misplaced, film was exposed, battery packs were unplugged so they weren't charged — nothing major, just annoying. But lately, things have gotten more serious. Yesterday there was a flood in the barn where equipment was being stored. Someone stuck a hose under the door and turned it on. It was clearly an attempt to destroy the equipment, or at least make it unusable for a while."

"You don't have any idea who might be behind this?" Barbie asked.

"No idea," Sam said. "And, of course, we don't want any bad publicity surrounding the film, so we can't bring in the authorities."

"Barbie can help!" Teresa exclaimed. "She's solved lots of mysteries!"

14

Sam smiled. "I know," he said. "That's exactly why I contacted the *Willow Gazette* and requested Barbie Roberts do a behind-the-scenes story. I'm hoping you'll agree to do a little extra work, Barbie."

Barbie could hardly contain her excitement. "It would be my pleasure, Sam," she said. "And don't worry, it won't be work at all!" If there was a mystery to be solved at Star Canyon Ranch, she was ready, willing, and eager to start the investigation!

Chapter 3

• • • • • • • • • • • • • • • • • • • •

NO QUIET ON THE SET

Just then, there was a loud cheer from the corral, and a voice called out, "Cut!"

"Oops!" Sam said. "Gotta get back to my place on the set. I'll meet you after this scene is wrapped up." He hurried to his position next to one of the cameramen.

A small group of actors gathered at the fence of the corral. They were all in costumes and makeup that Barbie knew would look completely natural on film. Dressed in leather chaps or jeans, cowboy boots, and wide-brimmed hats, they looked like a group one might see at a rodeo or a horse auction. They were waiting for instructions from a bearded man standing above them on a platform.

"He must be the director," Barbie said to Teresa.

"Okay," the man shouted through a bullhorn. "Take your places on the set. I want to shoot that scene again. This time, let's go through the whole thing, horse and all. Remember, you're cheering for the only rider who can handle the wildest horse in the canyon. Give it all you've got. Quiet on the set. Roll it!"

Barbie and Teresa stood by silently, watching the action begin. As directed, the group of cowboys cheered and kept their eyes on the doorway of the big indoor riding ring next to the corral. In seconds, a handsome, dark-haired actor with startling blue eyes came galloping through the doorway of the barn, riding the most beautiful black stallion Barbie and Teresa had ever seen.

"That's Orion!" Teresa whispered. "Isn't he amazing?"

A pure white star blazed from the center of the horse's forehead. As the stallion galloped to the center of the ring, his curly-haired rider pulled back on the reins and Orion raised his front legs in the air, throwing his mane to the wind. The rider threw his black hat in the air and smiled at the cheering crowd of onlookers.

17

"Perfect! Cut!" the director shouted. "Great job, Matt," he continued.

The actor smiled. "You're right," he said confidently. "I did do a great job, didn't I?"

"Easy with the ego, Matt," the director scolded the actor. Then he turned to a slim, tan woman dressed in jeans and a cowboy hat. "Annie, Orion seemed almost under control in that shot. Keep working with him. You can take him back to the stable now. We're done with him until this afternoon. Everyone, break for breakfast, and then we'll start shooting the scene in the hills."

The director climbed down from his perch on the platform and began talking with Sam Rogan.

Annie, the horse's handler, turned toward the corral while the handsome actor, still struggling to stay in the saddle, patted the horse's neck and tried unsuccessfully to quiet him. Just then, a girl wearing an apron rushed toward the horse. "Have a little sugar, Orion!" she called, holding out her hand.

Either the shrillness of the girl's voice or her sudden movement made the stallion buck, whinny,

18

and rear up again, his eyes white and wild with fear.

"Tillie! You silly fool! Get back!" shouted Annie. She rushed into the ring and roughly pulled the girl out of danger. "You have no business feeding that horse anything!" Annie shouted at the girl. "*Your* job on the set is to feed the cast and crew. *My* job is to take care of Orion!"

The girl was red-faced as Annie scolded her in front of everyone. She ran from the scene crying. Annie turned her attention back to the wild-eyed Orion, who was still bucking and rearing.

Barbie and Teresa watched from a safe distance as Matt Carson fought to stay in the saddle even as the horse pulled against the reins and tried to throw him off. To the amazement of everyone, the rider won the wild tug-of-war long enough to jump off and hand the reins to the horse's handler.

"Here you go, Annie," he said, a little breathless. "Take him. He's all yours. I don't think this animal is made to be around people. He's dangerous!"

"Listen," Annie replied gruffly. "This horse is a

star through and through. It's not Orion's fault. Too many things around here are making him skittish. Backfiring trucks, cameras flashing, and too many busybodies poking around trying to get a close look at him. From now on, nobody but me goes near him except during filming!" She led Orion away from the crowd and headed for Orion's special stable.

"Gee," the actor said, smoothing back his curly dark hair. "Doesn't she know I'm a star, too? That horse is wild!" He turned and spotted Barbie and Teresa for the first time. "Morning, ladies," he said, tipping his black hat and flashing a bright white smile at them.

"Allow me to introduce you," Sam Rogan said, coming up behind them. "Barbie and Teresa, meet Matt Carson, soon-to-be big star of the big screen!"

"If I live long enough," Matt Carson joked. "A few more wild rides like that one and I'll be done for! Of course, everyone seems to be more worried about how the horse is than how I might be after a ride like that. Nothing like playing second fiddle to an animal."

Barbie laughed, but she wondered if Matt was

jealous of the star treatment Orion was getting. "Well, at least you managed to stay in the saddle," she complimented the actor.

"Thanks," Matt replied. "I've been riding for a while, and I wanted to do my own stunts. Orion didn't take to me at first and Annie wasn't much help."

"True," Sam agreed. "Annie's not too keen on 'all this movie business,' as she calls it. If she had her way, she'd close down this production, load up Orion on that fancy trailer, and take him out of here. But she's just the handler, not the owner, and the owner knows movies are a good way to keep the money coming even when the champion's racing days are over."

"So," Matt said to Barbie, "you're the reporter-detective Sam talked about. Are you here as a reporter or a detective?"

"Maybe a little of both," Barbie replied.

"Well, there's no mystery here, I don't think, except the mystery of why a horse is getting more attention than I am."

Barbie and Teresa exchanged looks. Was the actor kidding, or was he really a little bit full of himself? "Say," Matt continued, "are you girls going to be around for a while? Maybe Sam and I could take you for a trail ride sometime. It's beautiful country around here, and there are plenty of horses in the stable that are easier to ride than Orion, that's for sure!"

"We'd love to," Barbie replied. He might be a little self-centered, but he sure was friendly. And there was a twinkle in his eyes Barbie found hard to resist.

"Well, how about this morning?" Sam suggested. "We'll have a couple of hours before the sun is too high in the sky. We aren't needed for filming until later. I'll call ahead and have four horses saddled up and ready for us. In the meantime, breakfast is on me," he said, pointing to a table covered with trays of scrambled eggs, sausage, bacon, pancakes, and three different kinds of juices.

Sam picked out a table in the shade and they sat together, eating a hearty breakfast. "We'll grab a bunch of boxed lunches to take with us on the trail," Sam said. "And then we'll get out of here."

"Speaking of getting out of here," Matt said, "I'll

go change out of this costume and catch up to you on the trail, okay?"

"Should we wait?" Barbie asked.

"No, that's all right," Matt replied quickly. "It could take a while to change and get the makeup off. I have to take care of a couple things, then I'll join you."

"Okay, my man," Sam said, clapping Matt on the back. "Ready to ride, girls?"

"Ready!" Barbie and Teresa said together.

"Let's do it!" Sam exclaimed.

Chapter 4

• • • • • • • • • • • • • • • • • • • •

TROUBLE AT STAR
CANYON RANCH

"Whoa!" Barbie commanded her horse as she slowed the gallop to a trot on the trail leading to the top of a hill. They'd been riding for more than an hour and a half. Sam had guided the way through trails that led to hidden streams, open canyons, and colorful rocky cliffs.

Matt caught up about half an hour into their ride. He was out of breath when he reached them. "Sorry I'm late," he apologized.

"Did you get everything taken care of?" Sam asked politely.

"Sure did," Matt said. "But hey, look at this view, will you?"

Matt was right. Nothing compared to the view

24

from the top, where the four horses lined up on the crest overlooking Star Canyon Ranch. The four trail riders took time out for lunch. Sandwiches, fruit, and drinks were plenty after the big breakfast they'd all eaten.

"It's beautiful up here!" Barbie sighed as she fed a piece of apple to her chocolate-brown bay, Mocha.

"We can see everything!" Teresa exclaimed, holding the reins of a golden palomino, Sunny.

"I didn't realize how big the ranch is," Barbie exclaimed. "Do all those acres belong to Star Canyon Ranch?"

"Everything up to the tree line over there," Sam said, pointing to the right. "Beyond that is another ranch called Roundup Ranch. It belonged to some old rodeo guy. The story is that the guy used to be a star on the rodeo circuit until he had a bad accident and had to quit riding. Without the money from the rodeo shows, he couldn't keep up the repairs on the place."

"I can see from here that the buildings look run-down," Barbie said.

"Oh, it's worse than run-down," Matt added. "Location scouts from Silvertone Studios came to this area looking for the right backdrop for filming. They tried to have a look at his place, but the front gate was chained up with a For Sale sign posted. The place is deserted. It turns out the rodeo guy passed away not too long ago."

"Yes, now that you mention it," Teresa agreed, "I don't see any movement down there at all."

"Nope," Sam said. "Nothing happening there, but I think things are going to start moving back at our ranch." He looked at his watch. "In fact, we've got to get moving ourselves. Shall we take the short way back and have a race, Teresa?"

"Great idea!" Teresa said. Then, without waiting for him, she turned Sunny around and took off like the wind.

"Hey!" Sam cried. "Wait for me!" He gave his horse a little nudge with the backs of his heels.

Matt and Barbie laughed as they turned their horses and began to follow. A flash of light coming from the deserted ranch caught Barbie's eye as she turned. "Hey, Matt! Wait!" she said, leaning forward in her saddle. "I saw something down there. Something shining or flashing like a light."

"Oh," Matt said, "it was probably just the sun reflecting on some loose metal."

"Hmmm," Barbie said, still staring at the spot by one of the buildings. "Maybe so." If she'd been alone, she would have ridden right down there and investigated for herself. But Teresa and Sam were already more than halfway down, and Barbie knew Matt had to get going, too.

Matt led the way and Barbie easily kept up with him. When they reached the bottom, Teresa ran out of the stable to meet them. "Oh, Barbie!" she cried. "Orion's gone! Everyone is going out to look for him. The stall door was open and Orion got out! No one knows how it happened. No one knows anything!"

Sam, Annie, and two other crew members gathered at the stables. They were all on horseback. Annie was shouting directions at them. "Spread out! Everyone split up!" she ordered. "Head for the hills! Look behind every rock and in every valley. We have to find him!"

"Let's help look for him," Barbie cried.

"Yeah, sure," Matt said. "We have to find him. After all, he's the star."

"We'll go together and split up when we get up the hill," Sam said, already leading the way.

This time, the girls knew the trail. When they came to a place where the trail offered choices, each of the four took a separate path. Sam turned left, Teresa went to the right, Barbie headed up, and Matt headed down. They agreed to meet back at the stable in an hour, with or without Orion.

Chapter 5

• • • • • • • • • • • • • • • • • • •

SURPRISING DISCOVERIES

Barbie rode slowly, pausing to listen for a whinny or any sound Orion might make. She studied the shrubbery off the path, looking for twigs and branches that could have been broken by a runaway horse. Finally, she reached the top of the hill again and took a moment to look around down below. From her position, she could see other searchers dotting the brush-covered hills on the other side of the Star Canyon Ranch. And on her right, there was the deserted Roundup Ranch. The roof of the main house was caving in on one side. One wall of the barn sagged and looked tired and old. The split-rail fence at the back was falling apart.

A warm breeze blew Barbie's hair across her eyes. When she tossed her head to brush it away from her face, she saw a flash of light just like she'd seen before. "I knew I saw something!" she whispered aloud.

Quickly, Barbie turned her head and tried to find the light again. Her horse seemed to read her mind. Mocha started slowly down the rocky hill, taking a route that was off the main trail. Barbie loosened her grip on the reins and let the horse carry her closer and closer to the other ranch. It was like a ghost town, empty and eerie.

There was no breeze at the bottom of the hill. The stillness of the air and the total silence made Barbie's throat tighten. Her mouth went dry as the horse clip-clopped slowly forward into unknown territory.

"It's okay, Mocha," Barbie said softly to her horse. "We're all right."

Naturally, Barbie was busy observing everything. She noticed the fresh FOR SALE sign on a small toolshed, and the back door of the ranch house was firmly shut. On the side of the barn there was a faded billboard that read ROUNDUP RANCH, HOME OF COWBOY PETE, RODEO CHAMPION. She noticed the rusted padlocks on the doors of the barn, another

30

small toolshed, and the back door of the ranch house firmly shut. And she noticed something else — fresh tire tracks in the dirt leading up to an old wooden garage.

Cautious but fearless, Barbie got off her horse, tied the reins around the fence post, and went forward on foot. As she approached, a blinding light hit her in the eyes. She squinted and followed the tracks to the light. It was coming from the door of the garage.

A shiny new brass key stuck in an old rusted, open padlock reflected the bright sunshine, throwing a beam of light up toward the rocky mountain Barbie had just come down. "It's not loose metal, it's this!" Barbie whispered.

Looking around to make sure she was really alone, Barbie carefully pulled the wooden door open. She was disappointed to find that the garage was empty. Barbie stepped in and saw that the wooden walls of the structure were covered with old rodeo programs and newspaper clippings that were yellowed with age. On the floor in the corner was a pile of more old programs.

Opening the door a little wider to let in the light,

31

Barbie looked closely at a program dated May 1976. There was a picture of a good-looking man identified as "Cowboy Pete" holding a silver cup he'd won for the roping event. In the picture with him were his young son and daughter. The headline read "Pete's Real Prizes." She then saw a newspaper article dated eleven years later that detailed a tragic event that injured Cowboy Pete. He'd been thrown from a horse during a steer-roping event and had broken a lot of bones. His rodeo days were over.

Barbie made some mental notes, planning to write them down later in her notebook: *Cowboy Pete, owner Roundup Ranch; died recently, ranch is deserted; new key/old lock; old newspapers and programs; tire marks leading to garage.*

Someone was definitely spending time at the abandoned ranch, and Barbie wondered if it might be the same person who was making trouble for the movie. She promised herself she'd come back here before the week was over.

Barbie turned to leave, but then she heard tires on the gravel down the long driveway toward the main house. She peeked through a crack in the wall of the garage and gasped. Coming slowly toward the garage was a rusty green pickup truck! It looked like the same one that had run the limousine off the road.

Barbie had to think fast — the driver of the green truck might be dangerous. Should she try to hide or run?

A whinny from Mocha at the broken fence told Barbie she had no choice. "I've got to make a run for it!" she whispered, bolting out the door.

Barbie jumped in the saddle and took off up the same trail she'd come down. When she was far enough away, she stopped behind a rock and looked down just in time to see the green truck pull into the garage. She waited to see who would come out of the garage. In seconds, a familiar figure emerged, closed the garage door, and snapped the padlock shut.

"Matt Carson?" Barbie gasped. "What's he doing there?"

Chapter 6

● ● ● ● ● ● ● ● ● ● ● ● ● ● ● ● ● ● ●

SNUBBED!

Confused about what she thought she had seen, Barbie took her time riding back to the ranch. She didn't want to think the worst about Matt Carson, but there was no doubt in her mind that the green pickup truck in the garage at Roundup Ranch was evidence that she needed to look at more closely.

So many thoughts and unanswered questions entered Barbie's mind. Mainly, she tried to make excuses that would remove her own suspicions about the handsome actor. Perhaps Matt had a perfectly good reason for being at the ranch. Maybe the green truck belonged to someone else. Maybe Matt had just borrowed it! But why would he borrow it and return it to Roundup Ranch? Nothing made any sense to Barbie.

34

As she rode slowly toward Star Canyon Ranch, Barbie heard Teresa calling her. "Barbie! Barbie! Where have you been?" her friend asked. "You were gone much longer than an hour. I was worried!"

"I'm sorry, Teresa," Barbie said sincerely. "I didn't mean to worry you."

"I've been looking all over for you," Teresa said. "I thought maybe you got lost in the hills. They found Orion grazing peacefully behind one of the barns. There he is, over there with everyone."

Barbie looked past Teresa and saw Orion bucking and rearing just as he'd done during filming.

"Thank goodness he's been found!" Barbie said. "I hope they'll be more careful with the stable door from now on."

"And what about Matt?" Barbie asked, thinking she already knew the answer since she'd seen him at Roundup Ranch.

"The last I heard, Sam was looking for Matt. He wanted him to meet with the writers," Teresa replied.

"Really? Isn't the script all written?" Barbie asked.

"That's what I thought, too," said Teresa. "But as

35

soon as Orion turned up missing, the director told the writers to start making Matt's part in the movie bigger. He didn't want to lose any more filming time waiting for Orion to show up. So for a little while it looked as if Matt was going to be the main star after all. But Orion is back, so I guess Matt's role will stay the same."

"Hmmm," Barbie murmured under her breath. "So if Orion is gone, Matt gets a bigger part in the movie? I wonder if he knows that."

"I guess he knows it if he's meeting with the writers," Teresa said.

"True," Barbie agreed, "but unless the writers are over at Roundup Ranch, he probably doesn't know."

"What?" Teresa said, totally confused.

Barbie started to explain, but was interrupted by the sound of Sam's voice calling to them from the stables. "Hey, you two! Want to trade your horses for a car? We'll be busy filming all day. I thought you two would like to see the town on your own."

"Actually," Teresa said to Barbie, "I think I've been out in the sun too long today. I'm afraid I might be getting a sunburn. I need to find a pharmacy to get some lotion. Do you mind?"

"Not at all," Barbie replied, still thinking about Roundup Ranch and Matt Carson. "I've had enough riding for today. Besides, I'm interested in seeing the town. Let's go."

The two friends rode back to the stables and turned in their horses, then picked up the car keys from Sam. Barbie drove down the long driveway to the main road. Signs led them into the small town of Sagebrush.

"Gee," Teresa said as Barbie steered the car down what seemed to be the only street in town. "There's not much of a town here."

Barbie laughed. "What do you mean? There's a movie theater, a general store, a gas station, a newspaper office, and a bank! What more could we ask for?"

"A pharmacy," Teresa reminded Barbie. "Lotion for my sunburn, remember?"

"Let's pull in at the gas station and ask if there's a shopping center nearby," Barbie said, pulling the car up by the door of the station. An unshaven man dressed in blue overalls and a cap with the name of an oil company on it came out.

"Excuse me," Barbie said to the man. "May I ask you a question?"

"Don't know as I can answer your question, but no harm in askin'," he replied in a friendly voice.

"We were wondering if there's a shopping center nearby," Barbie said.

"Well, we got the general store there," the man answered. "That's the center of shopping for most folks here. But you mean one of those strip malls or fancy shopping places? You must be with the movie folks over at the Star Canyon Ranch. Mighty glad to have you all here spending money in Sagebrush. You'll find everything you need at the general store."

"Thank you, sir," Barbie said with a smile. "We'll try it."

She waited for a tractor pulling a flatbed trailer full of hay bales to go by and then made a U-turn out of the gas station. They drove up the street and parked in front of the general store.

The man at the station was right. The store had everything from groceries to animal feed to pharmacy items. It even had a post office window at the back of the store, where a weathered old woman sat reading a newspaper.

While Teresa looked for her lotion, Barbie bought stamps from the old woman.

"You're a new face in town," the woman said in a crackling voice. "You with the movie folks?"

Barbie laughed. "I'm a newspaper reporter," she said, "but you're right. I am staying at Star Canyon Ranch with the movie company."

"Thought so," the woman said matter-of-factly. "I know everyone in this town, so I know who's new and who's not."

"Have you lived here all your life?" Barbie asked.

"Not yet," the woman joked. "But I've lived here up till now."

"So I guess you would have known Cowboy Pete, then, is that right?" Barbie said.

"Sure did," the woman replied. "Everybody knew Pete Flynn. He came to a sad end, but he sure was a star of the rodeo when he was still able."

"And do you know what will happen to his ranch?" Barbie continued.

"He left that ranch to his kids, but they don't live

there," the woman said. "Those kids never did amount to much," she said. "And that ranch hasn't seen a hammer or even a broom for a long time, even before Pete passed."

"Barbie?" Teresa called from another aisle.

"That's my friend looking for me," Barbie said to the woman. "It was nice talking to you. I'll see you again when I mail my letter."

"I'll be right here," the woman said, turning her attention back to her newspaper.

Barbie turned and walked to the front of the store where Teresa waited, holding a bag. "I got it," Teresa said, "and just in time. This sunburn is starting to hurt!"

"Oh, I'm sorry about that," Barbie said sympathetically. "We'll go right back to the ranch so you can put on some lotion."

The two friends went out to the car, and as they were about to get in, they saw Matt Carson and the cook-staff girl, Tillie, talking to the man at the gas station.

"Hi, Matt!" Teresa called out.

Both Matt and Tillie turned and looked down the street toward Teresa and Barbie. To their surprise, Tillie hurried inside the station, and Matt turned his back and walked the opposite way down the street!

"Hey!" Teresa said. "He didn't even say hello or wave!"

"And what was he doing with Tillie?" Barbie wondered.

"He acted like he didn't even see us!" Teresa added, surprised and a little hurt.

"Well," Barbie said, "maybe he's more stuck-up than we thought!"

Chapter 7

● ● ● ● ● ● ● ● ● ● ● ● ● ● ● ● ● ● ● ●

MEANWHILE, BACK AT
THE RANCH

"Well, at last we get to see the sunset," Barbie said as she turned the car into the gates of the Star Canyon Ranch. "Isn't that orange sky beautiful!"

"Everything looks so peaceful here," Teresa added. "You'd never know that there was so much excitement earlier in the day."

They returned the car and keys to the main ranch house and walked back to their own guest house. "Look!" Barbie exclaimed. "Someone has left us a note." An envelope addressed to Barbie and Teresa was taped to the front door. "I guess the excitement isn't over," Barbie said as she opened it and read what was inside. "We're invited to a cast and crew barbecue and campfire tonight. It's going to be held in the field in front

42

of the main ranch house and it starts in half an hour!"

"Oh, what fun!" Teresa said. "A real dude ranch campfire! And I have just the right shoes for it!"

"I'm sure you do." Barbie laughed. "From the weight of your suitcase I'd guess you could actually change your shoes a few times before the campfire burns out!"

"I wonder if Matt will be there," Teresa said as she rubbed the lotion in and then pulled a warm sweater over her head.

"I guess we'll find out soon enough," Barbie said, opening the front door and stepping out. "Listen, do you hear the music?"

Sounds of lively clapping in time to the music of a fiddle, a guitar, and a banjo filled the air. As the girls approached the field, the delicious smell of food cooking reached them along with the merry music. When they were close enough to see faces, Barbie recognized Tillie working by the open-pit barbecue, where three kinds of meat, corn on the cob, and kettles of beans sizzled, crackled, and bubbled.

Cast and crew danced, laughed, and sang as

they gathered around a glowing campfire. "It's a celebration!" Sam declared, coming up to Barbie and Teresa with a warm cup of coffee for each of them. "Orion is found, filming is going forward, and I think we're going to have a big hit movie on our hands when all is said and done!"

As Barbie looked around at the smiling faces of the crowd, she saw the director and all the actors and actresses who played cowboys, ranch hands, and townspeople. She saw Annie piling a plate high with barbecued ribs, corn, beans, and corn bread, and overheard her saying she'd just gotten back from searching for Orion and learned he'd already been found. But Barbie didn't see Matt Carson in the group.

"How about a dance, Ms. Roberts?" one of the extras in the cast asked Barbie. Before she could say yes or no, the actor whirled her around. The crowd formed a circle around them and clapped. Barbie got right into the spirit of it.

"How about it, Teresa?" Sam asked. "Shall we give Barbie and Buck a little competition?" He pulled Teresa into the circle, and she, too, danced with the glowing fire lighting her face.

Someone threw more wood on the fire and flames reached up and licked the starlit sky. The music swelled. The laughter and clapping grew louder and louder. Soon everyone was dancing while the cook staff clapped and "yee-hawed!" at the top of their lungs.

As Barbie's partner twirled her around, she caught a glimpse of Matt Carson walking outside the ring of people. "Hey, Matt!" Barbie cried, for- getting his earlier rudeness. "Come join the fun!"

Matt looked across the flames at Barbie and quickly turned away. Barbie couldn't believe it. Twice in one day, Matt Carson had snubbed her, and she had no idea why. She thought of leaving the barbecue and going after him to ask him face- to-face why he was avoiding her. And while she was at it, she wanted to ask him a few other ques- tions as well. What was he doing with the green truck? Why was he at Roundup Ranch? What was he doing in town with Tillie?

Before Barbie could decide whether to stay or go, a new song started and her partner twirled her around again. As the flames of the fire danced along with the crowd, someone yelled, "Fire! Fire!"

At first, no one reacted. It was hard to hear over the music. But in seconds the shouting voice grew louder and the words grew clearer. "Fire! Fire in the stable! Help!"

It was Annie, running across the field from the direction of the stable and shouting. All eyes turned toward the stables, but it wasn't the main stables that were engulfed in flames. It was Orion's stable, the one that was separated from the others, burning hot and bright across the open field.

"Oh, no!" Sam shouted. He was already on his cell phone calling for the Sagebrush Fire Department. "Star Canyon Ranch!" he yelled into the phone. "Fire in the stable! Hurry!"

Sam ran toward the burning building, as did all the rest of the cast and crew. People began passing buckets filled with sloshing water from hand to hand, then throwing them over the flames.

Annie wrapped herself in a water-soaked saddle blanket and ran into the burning stable screaming, "Orion! Orion!" In seconds she was outside again, coughing and wiping tears from her smoke-filled eyes. "He's gone! Orion is gone — again!" she shouted.

A siren signaled the arrival of a fire truck. The cast and crew stepped back and let the firefighters do their job. At last the fire was out and all that remained of Orion's private stable were ashes and embers that glowed the same color as the sunset.

For the second time that day, a search party formed to look for Orion, although it seemed hopeless to search the huge canyon area in the pitch-black night. There was nothing left for Barbie and Teresa to do except get a good night's sleep so they could join the search in the morning. They fell into bed, exhausted by the events of their first full day at the ranch.

As was her habit, Barbie stayed awake long enough to add more notes to her notebook. First she read over what she'd already written, then she added more names to her list.

Annie — Orion's handler; protective, doesn't like movie business, threatens to take Orion home.
Tillie — Cook talking to stranger; what is her connection to Matt Carson? Why were they in town together?

Matt Carson's name was already on her list. But next to his name, Barbie had a few notes to add:

Jealous of all the attention given to Orion — did Matt open stable door and let Orion get out? With Orion gone, Matt's part in the movie grows. Why was Matt Carson at Roundup Ranch?

Chapter 8

• • • • • • • • • • • • • • • • • • •

THE SECRET CANYON

The smell of bacon and eggs, hot biscuits, and sausage drifted in through the window of Barbie and Teresa's room on the early morning air. Along with the smell of food came the odor of wet ashes as a reminder of the terrible stable fire the night before.

Even before Barbie was out of bed, she saw the note slipped under the door of the guest house. Quietly, she crept out of bed and picked up the note.

Attention All Cast and Crew

Filming is canceled for today. All those capable of handling a horse are requested to join a search party to find Orion. Please meet at the

49

breakfast area by the stables by 7:30 A.M.
Thank you.

Sam Rogan
Assistant Director

Barbie looked at her watch. "Eight forty-five!" she gasped. "Teresa! Wake up! I'm afraid we've overslept."

Teresa opened her eyes and sat up. "Oh, no!" she said, looking at her arms. "My sunburn! I think it's going to turn into sun poisoning if I'm not careful! And it's so itchy! I'm afraid I'll have to stay in today. The only thing that helps this is to stay out of the sun."

Barbie looked at Teresa's arms and shook her head. "I guess you're right. No sun for you today."

"But I can always eat," Teresa said with a smile. "I'll walk over with you and have breakfast, and then I'll come back here and write some postcards."

The two friends walked over to the stables and asked for Mocha to be saddled up for Barbie. While waiting, they went to the food station that was always set up for the cast and crew. A group

50

of script writers was having a meeting at one table under an umbrella. They were so intent on their work they didn't even look up.

"Okay," one writer was saying, "we'll give this whole scene to Matt. Instead of being on horseback, we'll have him standing at the door of the barn talking to Buck. The camera will zoom in for a close-up, and Matt can deliver a long speech about saving the land. Sound good?"

The other writers agreed and made notes in their scripts.

"Gee," Teresa whispered to Barbie, "it sounds as if Matt is going to have a much bigger part now. I guess he'll be happy about that!"

"Yes," Barbie said, "he'll be the big star now for sure." She picked up a tray and handed one to Teresa.

Tillie was there, clearing things away for the next meal. She seemed unusually talkative and friendly to them. "You're up late, aren't you?" she said.

Barbie and Teresa nodded sheepishly. Tillie shook her head. "You missed everyone. They've all gone out looking for that horse again. Everyone acts like that horse is something so special, but I think the real star is Matt Carson. Even my brother thinks Matt's something special, and that's sayin' a lot since my brother doesn't usually pay much mind to show business and movie stars. He even wrote him a fan letter!"

"Well, I'm sure Matt Carson gets lots of fan letters, and he'll probably get even more after this movie," Barbie replied, taking a yogurt and a banana for her breakfast.

"So," Tillie went on, "you goin' out lookin' for that horse, too?"

"I'll have to try to catch up to the search party," Barbie replied politely.

"Well," Tillie said, shrugging her shoulders, "suit yourself. I don't know if I'd bother to help. That awful lady Annie isn't even looking for the horse."

"What do you mean?" Barbie asked.

"She took off in that fancy horse trailer early this morning before anyone was up except for us cook-staff folks," Tillie said. "Good riddance to her, if you ask me!"

Barbie and Teresa thanked Tillie for the breakfast, then ate quickly. "I'll see you later, Teresa,"

Barbie called to her friend. She jumped onto the saddle and rode toward the main trail.

There were no signs of any of the other searchers. Barbie rode the familiar trail and veered off down a path that looked less traveled. She followed it for a while until it opened onto a pasture hidden from easy sight from the main trail. Butterflies and hawks had already discovered the place, and it was silent except for the squawking of a hawk spying a field mouse or some other tiny prey. Barbie stopped and looked out over the field, admiring its stillness. But after a moment, the scene was disturbed by the sudden appearance of Orion walking out from behind a jagged rock formation!

Barbie steadied her own horse, hoping she could keep the bay from whinnying or snorting. She was sure absolute silence was needed if she was to have any luck at all in capturing Orion.

Barbie nudged Mocha's sides gently with her heels. Slowly, she guided her forward. Taking such careful steps made the field seem much wider. Orion was not steps away, he was acres away. Slowly, steadily, carefully, quietly, Barbie moved toward the unsuspecting stallion. She began to feel almost hopeful when suddenly, from behind the very rocks from which Orion had come, a lasso flew through the air and landed around Orion's neck!

Barbie was relieved to see Matt Carson holding the other end of the rope. She called out to him, wanting to help lead Orion back to the ranch. "Matt!" she shouted way across the field. "Hey, Matt!" She waved when he looked up, but Matt didn't wave back. Was she so far from him that he didn't recognize her? "It's me, Barbie Roberts!" she shouted as loud as she could.

For the third time, Matt Carson turned away from Barbie. He jumped onto Orion's bare back and headed in the opposite direction. But this time, Barbie was determined to follow him!

Chapter 9

• • • • • • • • • • • • • • • •

SURPRISE ENDING

Getting out of the secret canyon was not as easy as getting into it had been. Barbie went from a slow walk to a trot to a canter. Finally, she had to urge Mocha into a full gallop to keep Matt and Orion in sight. He led Barbie across a rocky dried-up creek. Mocha stumbled and kicked up loose stones. Fearing that the horse might pick up a rock in her hoof, Barbie was forced to slow down.

"Easy girl," she said soothingly. "Easy." The horse welcomed the slowing pace, and once they were trotting again, Barbie looked around to figure out where they were heading. At first, she thought she was riding toward Star Canyon Ranch. When she looked up at the sun and saw that it was behind her, she realized she was in fact heading in the opposite direction. Matt was leading her to the deserted Roundup Ranch!

It was no use calling after him again. Barbie knew the curly-haired rider was not going to answer her, nor was he going to stop and wait for her to catch up. She was sure now that Matt Carson had been plotting all along to get Orion out of the way so he could be the star of *Riding on the Wind.* She thought of turning back and getting Sam or someone else from Star Canyon Ranch to track Matt down. But then he might escape or possibly harm the valuable horse. So Barbie continued on alone.

At last she came to a ridge overlooking a familiar sight. Down below was Roundup Ranch, but Matt and Orion were nowhere in sight.

Barbie decided to sneak up on Matt on foot. She tied Mocha loosely to a tree trunk in a shady area. She poured water from a canteen into a leather pouch and hung it from a low limb so Mocha could drink. Then she crept down the hill, listening for some sound to follow. A whinny drifted across the grounds of the ranch. Barbie thought the sound came from somewhere near the garage, but as she got closer, she realized it was coming from the barn behind the garage.

Noiselessly, Barbie dashed forward and reached the garage. To her surprise, the door with the padlock was slightly open and the sound of paper rustling was coming from inside. Barbie leaned in, and before she knew what was happening, a force from behind shoved her forward. The door to the garage banged shut behind her. The rusty padlock snapped closed, and Barbie heard heavy footsteps walking away.

"Hey!" she shouted. "What are you doing, Matt? You won't get away with this. You've gone too far now."

There was no answer.

"Matt! Come back!" Barbie cried, throwing her shoulder against the door, trying to force it open. Old as the wood was, the door did not budge. She tried again, and this time fell backward against something metal. Even in the darkness Barbie knew it was the bumper of the green pickup truck.

The rustling sound that had first drawn her in grew louder. Barbie strained her eyes to see in the darkness without any luck. Something scampered

57

across her foot and then she knew what the rustling sound was. Mice were eating the old programs on the floor!

Another furry thing ran over her other foot, and Barbie shuddered. Trying to escape the rodents, Barbie struggled to open the rusted door to the truck. "At least I can get away from the mice," she said to herself as she jumped into the front seat. "Ouch!" she said. Her wrist banged against something hard on the seat. She felt around with her hands and grabbed onto a flashlight!

"At least something is going right," Barbie remarked. She pressed the switch and dim light flickered across the seat. To her surprise, a wallet and keys were also on the seat. Barbie opened the wallet and saw a driver's license. She read the name on the license: Liam Flynn. A photo above the name showed a curly-haired young man with a face surprisingly similar to someone with a different name — Matt Carson!

Suddenly, all the pieces clicked into place. It wasn't Matt Carson who had snubbed Teresa and her in town. It wasn't Matt Carson who had turned and run away from her at the barbecue. And it wasn't Matt Carson who had roped Orion and led the horse to Roundup Ranch. It was Liam Flynn, son of Cowboy Pete Flynn!

As the light went on in Barbie's head, light also poured in through the door to the garage that suddenly flew open. Barbie looked out the window and saw Liam Flynn looking in at her. Now that she was face-to-face with him, she could see that his smile was a little cruel, not open and friendly like Matt Carson's. His eyes were not blue but were cloudy gray and framed by heavy brows. Quickly, Barbie locked the truck's doors to keep him out and started rolling up her window.

"So we meet at last, Miss Big-time Reporter," Liam Flynn growled through the window. "But you're not going to ruin my plans now that I've finally got my hands on the horse. I've already sent the ransom note demanding two million dollars for his return. By now my sister will have delivered it, thinking she was just delivering a fan letter from her dear brother, Liam. Poor Tillie, she was always the stupid one."

Barbie wanted to keep him talking while she tried to think of a way out of this mess. "So it was you who caused all the trouble on the set? The flood, the fire, the open stable door?"

Liam flashed his jagged teeth and laughed. "Of course it was me," he said. "When those movie folks first came to town, Tillie got a job with the cook staff. She told me I look a lot like the star. So at first I was just having a little fun messing up stuff on the set. If anyone saw me on the ranch, they just thought I was Matt. Then I found out about Orion and realized there was more than fun in it for me — there was big money!"

While Liam bragged, Barbie slowly picked up the keys from the seat and inserted one into the ignition. Quietly, Barbie turned the key. She surprised her captor completely when she threw the gear into reverse, stepped on the gas, and rammed the green pickup backward through the garage door!

Liam Flynn fell backward. Before he could get up, Barbie turned the truck toward the main road and roared away from Roundup Ranch. Breathless and trying to keep control of the steering wheel with all her might, she turned onto the main road. To her horror, Barbie just missed a head-on collision with a black limousine! The sleek black car veered off the road and into the ditch. Knowing she'd caused a terrible accident, Barbie stopped the truck, got out, and ran back to where the limousine had taken a slight nosedive into a soft shoulder of the road.

"You!" Ralph, the limousine driver, exclaimed as he climbed out of the driver's seat.

"What are you doing, Barbie?" Matt Carson cried, opening the back door of the limo.

"I . . . I . . ." Before she could explain, a flashing light and siren rushed toward them and a police car pulled up.

"Is anyone hurt?" the officer asked.

"Officer!" Barbie cried. "Hurry! There's a thief at Roundup Ranch!"

As Barbie rushed to explain, she, Ralph, and Matt jumped into the police car with the officer and headed back toward Roundup Ranch. There was Annie driving Orion's fancy horse trailer toward Star Canyon. Liam Flynn was right in front of her, struggling to stay on Orion's back as he tried to race away.

Realizing that his attempts were hopeless, Liam jumped off the horse and ran for the hills. "That's him!" Barbie shouted to the police officer.

Matt and the officer were already in hot pursuit. Racing past the garage, they jumped over the rotting fence and ran down the rocky trail. Finally, the two of them caught up to Liam Flynn. He fought to escape, but it was no use. While Matt held him to the ground, the officer snapped handcuffs around his wrists and led him back to the squad car.

At the same time, Annie had caught up to the horse that Liam had abandoned. "Orion!" Annie cried happily. "You're back!" She talked to the horse as though it was a long-lost friend. "And I've got your trailer all clean and ready for you," she explained to the stallion. "No, I wouldn't let a champion get into a trailer that wasn't freshly washed, would I? No."

Barbie smiled. She had never heard Annie sound so sweet!

Gradually, the story unfolded. Barbie took careful notes as each piece of the puzzle fell into place. Annie had taken Orion's trailer to be washed after ashes from the fire at the stable had covered it.

62

Matt had gone to New York for another audition and was just returning from the airport in the limousine. And Tillie hadn't had a chance to deliver the ransom note to Matt.

Teresa was there when Mocha came back to the stable without Barbie. The horse had gotten loose and returned to the ranch. She and Sam were just about to go looking for her when the limousine, and Orion's fancy trailer, came up the driveway to Star Canyon Ranch.

Later that evening, Barbie and Matt and Teresa and Sam joined the whole cast and crew for a celebration cookout.

"Wow, Barbie," Teresa said to her friend, "things turned out so perfectly. Liam Flynn is in jail, and *Riding on the Wind* is going to make Orion and Matt Carson big, big stars."

"Hear, hear!" Matt Carson said, flashing that bright white smile right at Barbie. "But the true credit goes to the real star on the set, Ms. Barbie Roberts, reporter, detective, friend!"

63

Barbie's Reporter's Notebook

Can YOU solve *The Mystery of the Missing Stallion*? Read the notes in Barbie's reporter's notebook. Collect more notes of your own. Then YOU solve it!

Story Assignment: The filming of a new movie, *Riding on the Wind,* is taking place on location at Star Canyon Ranch. Do a behind-the-scenes story of the filming.

● ●

Background Info

● Matt Carson, a young actor who hopes this movie will make him a big star

● Orion, a black stallion, retired champion race-horse, who has top billing over Matt Carson

● Trouble on the set started out small, soon became dangerous — flood, fire, Orion missing

● Roundup Ranch next door, deserted, once owned by Cowboy Pete, rodeo champ injured and forced out of rodeo; ranch is falling apart

The Mystery

Who: Who is causing all the trouble on the set?

What: What does anyone have to gain from bad publicity, stealing Orion, ruining the movie?

How: How does Barbie learn the truth?

Where: Where is Orion?

Why: Why is Matt Carson snubbing Barbie?

Write in the facts and clues you detected in the story. Here are a few to get you started.

• A green pickup truck tries to run the limousine carrying Barbie and Teresa off the road.

• The horse disappears after Tillie has already frightened the horse and Annie yelled at her for it.

_____

_____

_____

_____

_____

_____

_____

_____

_____

_____

Jot down the suspects in the case:

_____

_____

_____

_____

_____

_____

_____

_____

_____

_____

_____

_____

_____

_____

_____

_____

_____

_____

_____

_____

_____

_____

_____

_____

_____

Now YOU solve it! Write down the name of the culprit and why you think you have the right person.

_____

_____

_____

_____

_____

_____

_____

_____

_____

_____

_____

_____

_____

_____

_____

_____

_____

_____

_____

_____

_____

CONGRATULATIONS from BARBIE! You are an official star reporter. Sharpen your mystery-solving wits and get ready to help Barbie solve her other big cases, *The Haunted Mansion Mystery, The Mystery of the Jeweled Mask,* and *Mystery Unplugged.*

72